For everyone who has had to leave.

Copyright © 2012 by Magikon forlag, www.magikon.no
Text: Veronica Salinas, www.salinas.no
Illustrations: Camilla Engman, www.camillaengman.com
Translation: Jeanne Eirheim

Published in Canada and the USA in 2013 by Groundwood Books

Groundwood Books / House of Anansi Press
110 Spadina Avenue, Suite 801, Toronto, Ontario M5V 2K4
or c/o Publishers Group West
1700 Fourth Street, Berkeley, CA 94710

We acknowledge for their financial support of our publishing program the Government of Canada through the Canada Book Fund (CBF).

Library and Archives Canada Cataloguing in Publication
Salinas, Veronica
The voyage / written by Veronica Salinas ; illustrated by
Camilla Engman ; translated by Jeanne Eirheim.
Translation of: Reisen.
Issued also in electronic format.
ISBN 978-1-55498-386-5
1. Ducks—Juvenile fiction. I. Engman, Camilla II. Title.
PZ7.S233Vo 2013   j839.82'38   C2013-900848-9

The illustrations were drawn by hand and composed and colored digitally.
Printed and bound in China

The Voyage

Veronica Salinas

Illustrations by Camilla Engman

Translation by Jeanne Eirheim

Groundwood Books   House of Anansi Press   Toronto   Berkeley

Maybe one day you have to leave.

And you are blown so far that you forget
who you are and where you come from.

And you land someplace.

You think it's strange there.

And you wait and wait and wait for something to happen.

And suddenly a fly comes along and you ask the fly, "Do you know who I am?"

And the fly says something you do not understand.

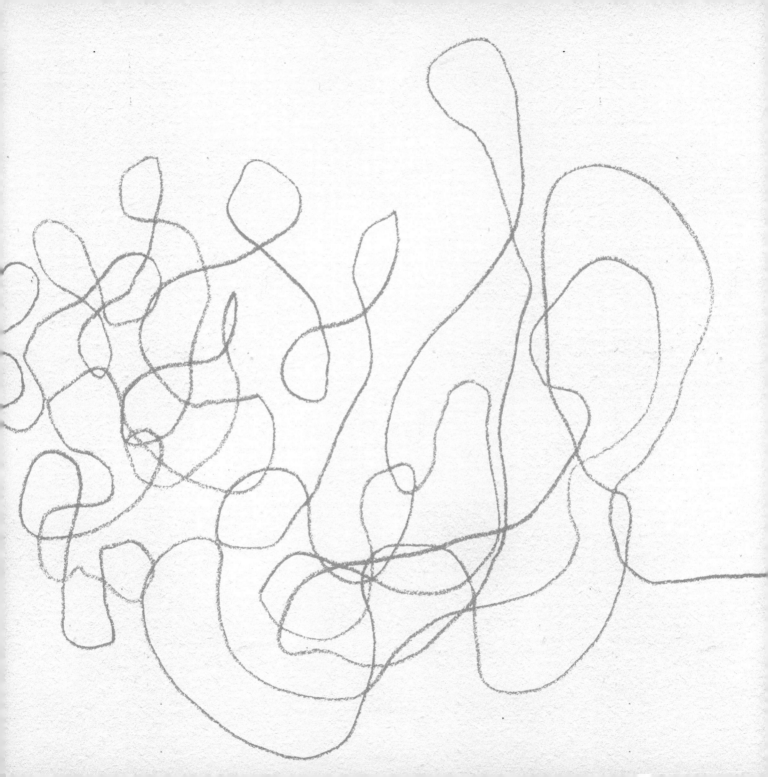

And later a fish comes along and you say, "Perhaps you know who I am?"

And the fish says something you do not understand.

And then a mouse comes along and you ask eagerly, "Who am I?"

And the mouse also says something you do not understand.

And you are sad because no one is saying anything you can understand.

But then somebody with big feet comes along, and although you do not know who it is, you see that it is someone who looks a little like you. And quickly you ask, "Who am I?"

And the other one laughs and says, "You are who you are."

"And me? What about me?" asks the one with big feet.

And you say, "You are who you are." And you laugh and play, and you are so happy because the other one understands the game, and because it has said something you understand.

And before long you understand what the fly is saying and what the fish is saying and what the mouse is saying.

And you just laugh because everything seems so
easy now. The flowers bloom, the sand tickles
your feet, and the sun is shining upon you.

And one day while you are playing, a strong wind comes, and
you see the flowers blow away and the sand blow away. And you
see the other one blow away, too, just as you were blown away
yourself, and you stand there holding on while the wind blows and
blows and blows.

And after a while the wind dies down
and you are standing alone.

And sure enough, someone else comes along and says, "Hello," and now you can say, "Hello," too.

And because now you understand, you can say, "I am me. And you? Who are you?"